THE TOY PARTY

AN EROTIC ADVENTURE

VICTORIA RUSH

VOLUME 15

JADE'S EROTIC ADVENTURES - BOOK 15

COPYRIGHT

The Toy Party © 2019 Victoria Rush

Cover Design © 2019 PhotoMaras

❀ Created with Vellum

FEEL THE RUSH:

Jade's Erotic Adventures – Book 1

When lonely divorcée Jade seeks to broaden her horizons, she's invited to a private dinner event which promises to stimulate all of her senses. Wearing nothing but masquerade masks, dinner guests receive special service under the table while their fellow diners look on...

The Dinner Party

Jade's Erotic Adventures - Book 2

Jade discovers an exotic adventure club where strangers meet to explore each other's bodies in mysterious dark rooms. Using special effects to project swirling light patterns onto their figures, the shifting shadows provide just enough illumination to highlight their naked bodies while protecting their identities...

The Dark Room

Jade's Erotic Adventures - Book 3

Jade discovers a yoga club where members stretch and explore each other's bodies in the buff. She books an appointment, and during the first session meets a young redhead who tantalizes her with her flexibility and stunning body...

Naked Yoga

For the uninhibited...

1

———

"How goes the practice?" I asked my best friend and certified sex therapist, Hannah, over lunch. "Any interesting new cases?"

We were meeting for our weekly catch-up at our favorite restaurant on Chicago's Navy Pier overlooking Lake Michigan. With our busy schedules, it wasn't always easy for us to find time to nurture our longstanding friendship. But I could always count on Hannah to share some juicy tidbits from her private practice during our two-hour break every Wednesday.

"Never a dull moment," she said. "You'd be surprised at the endless variety of dysfunctions people come to me with. Just yesterday, I had a young woman worried about her excessive squirting when she orgasms."

"Is that a problem?" I said. "I mean, isn't that a *good* thing? I squirt sometimes when I come too, but it's usually after a long buildup and during an unusually powerful orgasm. Most of my partners find it to be a huge turn-on."

"That's what I tried to tell her. I explained that it's perfectly natural for many women and that she shouldn't worry about it. She thought she was literally peeing on her partners during sex."

I choked on a salad crouton in mid-swallow and quickly washed it down with a gulp of water.

"Just to be clear, though—it's *not*, right? There's a lot of misconceptions about vaginal squirting. I don't want to feel self-conscious about it—"

"No," Hannah chuckled. "You needn't worry about spraying your lover with an unintended golden shower. Ninety percent of the time, it's just the ejection of your natural lubrication when your vagina contracts during orgasm. As you suggested, whenever it happens it's usually a sign of exceptional internal wetness and/or unusually strong contractions."

"And the other ten percent of the time?"

"Some women expel a secretion from the Skene's glands, located next to the urethra. And yes, in very rare circumstances, one can become temporarily incontinent and expel a small amount of urine. But it's all healthy organic fluid, and in all cases an indicator of a powerful orgasm. Most women should be thrilled to experience that kind of 'dysfunction'. The more common problem is the lack of ability to orgasm at all."

"Really?" I said, watching some dark clouds roll in from the east side of the bay. "I thought that was mostly limited to heterosexual couples where the man doesn't know how to properly stimulate his partner."

"That's common, yes. Most guys can't find a woman's clit with a magnifying glass. But honestly, most of the time it's because the woman has some kind of mental block. Either she grew up learning sex was something to be ashamed of or she had an early traumatic experience. The latest studies show that seventy-five percent of women can't orgasm from intercourse alone and up to fifteen percent can't come at all."

"How do you help them overcome their problem, if you don't mind my little play on words."

"Actually, that boils it down to the core of the problem. They have to learn how to break down the barriers stopping them from achieving climax. First, I teach them that pleasure is a natural part of the sexual experience, designed to encourage procreation. Then I tell them the best way to experience orgasm is to stop trying to orgasm. It's like a guy who can't get it up when the chips are down—they're feeling too much pressure to perform. I encourage them to find a quiet place where they can explore their bodies without any distractions then lose themselves in the journey of discovery without worrying about the destination."

"Alone?"

"At first, yes. There are too many expectations when you bring a partner into the equation. They have to learn how to break down the walls restricting their freedom of expression before they can let others into their intimate space."

I nodded, reflecting back on my own first time experiencing sexual pleasure. It was when I was taking a bath and I discovered how good it felt to let the water from the faucet flow over my pussy. From that day forward, I experimented with endless types of self-stimulation. By the time I had my first fling with a high school boyfriend, all my hang-ups about sex had been thoroughly dispelled.

"What about when they return to their sexual partners? Is there even such a thing as a vaginal orgasm? What happens to the *other* seventy-five percent who can't come with their husbands?"

"That whole vaginal vs. clitoral orgasm concept that Freud first introduced is a total myth," Hannah said. "It wasn't until about twenty years ago that scientists properly mapped the full anatomy of the clitoris. Did you know that over ninety percent of the clitoral structure is actually *inside* the vagina? The tiny glans and shaft on the outside are just the parts that we can see. There's no reason why a woman can't experience a penetrative orgasm if properly aroused and stimulated by a caring partner."

The sun suddenly broke through a hole in the clouds, casting a spotlight over the nearby grounds in Millennium Park. The chrome skin of the famous bean-shaped sculpture glistened in the light, reminding me of my favorite U-shaped vibrator.

"Is that what happens when we stimulate the G-spot?"

"Partly. The G-spot corresponds to the location of the underside of the shaft of the clitoris. It's a bit like the sensitive frenulum on the underside of a man's penis. But the rest of the clitoral structure surrounds much of the vagina, which is why it feels good even when we're having missionary sex. We're all born with the same genital anatomy. It's not until around the third month of prenatal development that the structures deviate into the familiar male and female forms."

My panties began to dampen as I began to think about all the new ways I could explore my pussy with my large collection of vibrating dildos.

"Fascinating," I said, shifting restlessly in my seat. "Do you ever encourage your clients to experiment with *sex toys* to mix things up if they're still having trouble making it work?"

"After a while, yes. But first they have to get in the right frame of mind. It's not an exaggeration to say that the brain is the largest sex organ. A lot of women can actually *think* themselves to orgasm. You've got to be *mentally* aroused before you can achieve physical excitement. I don't want my clients to become too dependent on the artificial stimulation of a sex toy before learning to enjoy sex the natural way. No partner can hope to match the intensely focused stimulation of a sex toy. At its core, sex is designed to be a social activity to ensure procreation."

I slammed my knife and fork on my plate and stared at Hannah in mock indignation.

"Don't tell me you're one of those sexist shrinks who still believes sex is only meant to be enjoyed between a man and a woman under holy matrimony."

"Of course not. We humans have thankfully evolved to the point where we can enjoy sex for its own sake. You know me better than that. I consider myself to be pansexual. I enjoy and encourage all forms of sexual expression. Gay, straight, bi, transgender—whatever turns your crank. Life's too short to be worried about all that hypocrisy about only one proper way to experience sex. So if using toys helps you spice up your sex life and keeps your relationships fresh and exciting, I'm all for it."

"Cheers to that," I said, raising my glass of sangria.

"To *hump day*," Hannah winked, clinking her glass against mine.

"You know, all this discussion has got me thinking. I feel like I've grown so much since my boring marriage ended a few years ago. My sex life is so much more enjoyable now that I'm open to having sex with other women. And my house is a veritable sex toy museum. I've often thought about inviting some of my closest friends over for a toy party. You know—to share the *wealth*, as it were. Would you be willing to give a little talk about some of your insights on sexual health? I'm sure there's a lot of other women who could benefit from your knowledge and experience."

Hannah peered across the table at me with a raised eyebrow.

"Were you intending for this to be a 'hands on' party, or just an educational meeting?"

I paused as a small curl formed at the edge of my lips.

"I was thinking we could start out as an informational forum and see where it goes from there. You could share your knowledge of sexual anatomy and mental health while I demonstrate the latest advances in sex toy development. If some of the ladies want to practice some of their learnings and avail themselves of the available sex aids, I don't see why we should want to stop them. Are you down for that?"

Hannah took another sip of her wine as she peered over the rim of her glass with fluttering eyes.

"Sounds like it could be fun. Knowing you, I have a feeling this little party will soon devolve into a full-blown orgy. But I've never experienced one of those, so count me in."

"Good," I said. "I'll send out the invites later today. Are you available next Saturday?"

Hannah reached into her purse and pulled out her phone. I could tell even before she checked her schedule from the way she was squirming in her chair that she was already committed. She tapped the screen twice then looked up at me and smiled.

"I think I can make that work."

I could barely contain my excitement on the drive home thinking about how I would organize our get-together for maximum enjoyment. Part of me was genuinely looking forward to educating my friends about all the cool sex toys

I'd discovered in my journey of sexual exploration since my divorce. But I definitely had another agenda. There were a few girls I'd had my eye on for some time who'd rebuffed my subtle advances. Whether it was because they professed to be 'happily married' or because they just weren't into lesbian sex, I had a feeling this party would tear down whatever remaining walls they might have to expanding their sex lives.

I knew full well that some of the toys I'd be demonstrating would tempt more than one fence-sitter into wanting to try them out right then and there. I just had to create the right atmosphere. By the time I pulled into my driveway, my car seat was soaked in a puddle of wetness under my burning crotch. I raced upstairs and flipped open my laptop, starting a new email message with the subject *Girl's Slumber Party*. With trembling hands, I began composing my message:

Dear friends,

This Saturday, I'll be hosting a most unusual and exciting party. The theme of the gathering is 'sexual health and wellness'. I've invited my good friend and registered sex therapist, Hannah Bristol, to give an informative presentation on the latest developments in the area of women's sexual health.

A big part of this is learning to relax and explore our bodies in a safe and nurturing environment. To this end, I've invited another friend, Cheryl Clifton from the local branch of the Babeland adult emporium chain to demonstrate some of the exciting new sex toys they've recently introduced. You're encouraged to learn, experiment, and dabble to the extent you feel comfortable.

This is a girls-only party. Leave your husbands, boyfriends, and other cockadoodles at home. Dress comfortably—it'll be our own little slumber party. Come one, come all!

RSVP by Friday p.m.

See you all soon,

Jade xo

As I began to fill in the To: field with the email addresses of my friends and associates, I paused after entering the names of the obvious candidates. It went without saying that I would invite the women I'd already shared a private tryst with and those who I knew to be lesbians. But half the fun would be trying to entice my stanch heterosexual friends to drop their britches along with everyone else.

By the time I finished filling in the list of addressees, I'd assembled an eclectic list of twenty friends and acquaintances, all of whom I'd be happy to fuck at the slightest provocation. I paused for only a millisecond before tapping the Send button. Then I tore off my pants and plunged my favorite rabbit vibrator dildo deep into my pussy. As I slid down in my chair spreading my legs wide apart, I closed my eyes imagining what it would be like to watch twenty sexy women pleasuring themselves while the rest of us looked on.

2

———

By Saturday afternoon, I was already dripping in anticipation of the coming festivities. Almost everyone I'd invited had RSVP'd that they were planning to attend. The only person I still hadn't heard from was the hot housewife who lived on the opposite side of my back yard. I'd caught Alana stealing lingering glances at me from her upper deck whenever I lay around my pool in my bikini. But her needy husband always seemed to be hanging about, and we'd never managed to find any private time together. Tonight, I had a special plan for how I might entice her over to my place.

I'd arranged the guest chairs in a semicircle in the middle of my family room, with two additional chairs in front of the arc, facing the backyard window. One of the chairs would be reserved for the official presenter—first Hannah, then Cheryl. I would sit in the second chair providing color commentary. But most of the 'commentary' I was planning to provide would be more *visual* than verbal. I knew the only way I was likely to get the rest of the women to sample the vibrators would be if I demonstrated how some of them worked myself.

There wouldn't be enough replicas of each vibrator for every participant to try them at the same time, but between the many different types we were planning to show, there'd be more than enough to keep everyone entertained. And unlike most other sex toy shops' policy of offering no returns of purchased products for hygienic reasons, each woman at *our* party would be welcome to share and pass along their toys for the pleasure of the other participants.

Beside each chair, I'd placed a container of alcohol wipes and a fresh towelette so everyone could safely clean each device before reuse. I didn't want anything stopping the ladies from being willing to experiment and enjoying themselves to the fullest. The last thing I did to set the mood was draw the drapes and turn the dimmer switch down. I wanted just enough light to create a playful atmosphere while still providing enough visibility for everyone to watch one another.

In front of my own chair, I left the curtains parted a small crack with a direct line of sight to Alana's balcony. There wouldn't be enough space for someone outside my fenced yard to make out what was going inside with an unaided eye. But using the spyglass I'd often caught Alana using behind her kitchen window, she'd be able to zoom in on the action all she wanted. After dusk, the light from inside my house would create the effect of an illuminated stage in a darkened theater. Everybody else's privacy would be safely protected facing away from the window. But Alana would have a bird's-eye view of me displaying all of my favorite toys.

As my friends began to arrive, we shared some wine and cheese and made small talk about the latest developments in our work and personal lives. Nobody wanted to broach the subject of our planned activities for later in the evening, but by the time the last attendee arrived, everybody was nicely loosened up by the free-flowing alcohol. I invited everyone to take a seat in the semicircle, while Hannah and I took adjacent chairs facing the group. Hannah had brought a small case with her that she placed it on the floor beside her chair.

"Good evening everyone and welcome to our little get-together," I said. "It's great to see all my close friends together once again. We seem to find it more and more diffi-cult these days to make time to commune with our busy schedules. We've got an interesting theme for tonight's gath-ering, and I've invited two close friends to make a presenta-tion in the context of women's sexual health. I think you'll find the planned festivities will be both mentally and physi-cally stimulating."

As I began to make eye contact with the women around the room, they smiled nervously back at me. I was sure many of them had no idea what they were getting them-selves into.

"Some of you already know Hannah, a registered sex therapist who has been counseling women in her private practice for almost ten years. I think you'll find she has some interesting insights and experiences to share with us. I've also invited my good friend Cheryl Clifton, who is the owner of the Chicago Babeland adult store on Michigan Avenue, to show us some of the fascinating new sex toys that have recently come to market."

I glanced toward Cheryl and she raised her arm to acknowledge her presence. Some of the ladies nodded toward her, recognizing her from their previous trips into her store.

"Hannah," I said, who was sitting beside me. "Did you want to start things off with a few opening comments?"

"Thanks, Jade," Hannah smiled. "Jade and I were talking the other day over lunch about some of the concerns many women still have about their sexual health. She thought it might be fun to share some of our mutual experiences and learnings in a safe and learning environment."

She reached down and opened the case beside her and pulled out an unusually shaped stuffed toy.

"I didn't want to get overly formal about what should be a fun subject, so I thought I'd try to lighten the mood using my favorite puppet."

She placed her right hand in the back of the stuffed toy then held it up for the whole room to see. Many of the women giggled when they recognized the familiar shape and features of a woman's vulva.

"Hi, I'm Valerie, the vagina puppet," Hannah squeaked in a playful voice. "While I may not be proportioned to the correct relative scale, I think you might recognize some of the familiar features on my body."

Hannah caressed the velvety sides of the puppet framing the organ like two puffy parentheses.

"These are the labia majora," she said. "Their job is to cover and protect the more sensitive internal parts of the vagina. Though I must say I rather enjoy having this part of me stroked and caressed as a prelude to deeper exploration of my body."

Many of the women around the circle chuckled as they watched Hannah playing with her puppet. But they shifted uncomfortably in their seats as her fingers moved closer toward the inside of the faux vulva.

"These thinner folds are the labia minora. They're even more sensitive to touch than my larger siblings and can get quite wet when properly stimulated. Their purpose is mostly to provide a slippery surface for easy penetration of a man's penis, but I like to insert *other* phallic-shaped devices inside me when the mood strikes. These lips also connect at their top edge to the clitoris and help provide some very pleasant friction during vaginal thrusting."

Hannah placed the fingers of her left hand over a puffy red ball at the apex of the inner folds. Then she flipped up a flap of silk covering the nub and smiled.

"And this is the hood of the clitoris that helps protect this super-sensitive organ when it is not in use."

She pinched the fingers of her left hand together and inserted them into the opening of the vulva, thrusting her hand gently in and out. The silky hood of the clitoris pulled back and forth over the nub as she stroked her pretend pussy.

"Notice how the hood pulls forward and back over the glans as the labia minora are stretched and contracted with each penetration."

Some of the ladies around the arc crossed their legs and squeezed their thighs excitedly together, becoming aroused by the vivid depiction of their private anatomy.

"Many women think they can't come just from penetrative sex," Hannah continued. "But this design is intended to increase the stimulation on our most sensitive organ even from indirect touching. Did you know that the clitoris is the only organ in either a man's or a woman's body with the sole purpose of providing pleasure? And that the head of the clitoris has over *seven thousand* nerve endings—even more than in the glans of a man's penis? So much for penis envy. If guys had any idea how good it feels to stimulate a woman's clit, they'd gladly switch places with us."

Everyone in the group laughed out loud and nodded in agreement, starting to loosen up.

"But here's the really interesting part," Hannah said as she angled her puppet from side to side for all the women to see. Surrounding the vulva behind each of the labia majora were two puffy 'wings' connected to the outside shaft of the clitoris, making it look like an inverted wishbone.

"The clitoris is actually far larger than many of us believe. The little nub and shaft on the outside is just the tip of the iceberg."

She lifted the two wings framing the internal walls of the vagina to reveal a larger pair of puffy tissues.

"These tissues extend inside and around the walls of the vagina and connect directly to the clitoral shaft and glans. The thinner flaps are called the *crura*, and the puffier tissues underneath them are the *bulbs*, corresponding in many ways to the corpora cavernosa in the shaft of a man's penis. They're all part of the greater clitoral structure, extending more than four inches around each side of the vaginal wall at rest."

Many of the ladies leaned in closer as their eyes widened in surprise, realizing for the first time just how large and all-encompassing this sensitive part of their anatomy was.

"The male and female genitalia both develop from the same embryonic structures," Hannah continued. "They don't actually differentiate until fairly late in fetal development. Just like a man's penis, these structures swell and extend fifty to three hundred percent when stimulated. So the next time someone tells you there's no such thing as a vaginal orgasm, don't believe it. A woman should be able to come just as easily from proper internal stimulation as from external manipulation of the outside glans."

Recognizing that some of the women were eager for the next phase of the demonstration, I signaled to Hannah that it was time for a shift in the discussion.

"Thank you, Hannah, for that entertaining and enlightening explanation of a woman's sexual anatomy. I don't know about you guys, but I'm feeling a lot more empowered about my sexual health knowing that my lady cock is just as big and powerful as any man's."

The women around the circle cheered and clapped their hands excitedly, equally surprised and impressed with Hannah's presentation.

"What do you say we put Valerie away for a little while and focus on learning some the interesting ways we can stimulate our *real* peachkas now that we understand a little better where all the interesting parts are?" I nodded toward Cheryl and she switched places with Hannah, placing a much larger case on the floor in front of her. "Cheryl is now going to demonstrate the almost infinite varieties of toys we can use to stimulate our wonderful flower in the privacy of our own homes."

"Or with a partner," Cheryl suggested. "I think you'll find these sex aids are equally stimulating used either alone or as part of communal play. There's no reason why you shouldn't be able to introduce some of these toys into your partnered sex life to keep it vibrant and interesting."

I smiled at her and winked, happy that she'd planted the seed for broader group exploration.

She reached down and flipped open her case. Inside, was a treasure trove of multicolored and unusually shaped toys. She picked up two phallic-looking objects of different sizes.

"Following on Hannah's illumination of the shape and

structure of the clitoris," she said. "Women's sex toys fall into two general categories: internal and external."

She held up the smaller object and turned it around in her hand for everyone to see.

"This little guy may look familiar to many of you as the trusty 'pocket rocket' vibrator. It's only about two inches long and less than an inch in diameter, but it packs quite a wallop for its small size."

Cheryl ran her fingers teasingly over the nubby end of the finger-sized device.

"You can place these ridges overtop of your clit and twist the tube to select one of three different vibration settings."

She twisted the shaft of the pocket rocket and the device began to hum with a soft whine.

"The good news is that you can carry this guy around in your smallest purse and use it fairly discreetly, since it's no bigger than your index finger."

She pulled two more pocket rockets out of her case and handed them to the women at opposite ends of the semicircle.

"Feel free to pass these around and see what they feel like as you experiment with the different settings. This is what I like to call our 'entry-level' vibrator. It's very basic, but it definitely does the job."

I pulled my own pocket rocket out of the pocket of my jeans and placed it playfully between my crotch.

"If any of you want to see what it actually feels like against your clit," I said, "don't be shy about giving it a try. Clothes on or off, this is a judgement-free zone. We're all liberated ladies here and I don't want anybody to feel self-conscious about enjoying each of these toys to their fullest limits. You'll notice that I've placed some alcohol wipes and clean towels beside every chair, so you can safely and comfortably clean each device after each use."

"And that's another point I want to make about sex toys in general," Cheryl chimed in. "Different toys are made out of different materials. But some are more *hygienic* than others. You should always buy toys made out of medical-grade silicone or hard plastic. Avoid any device made out of a soft jelly or rubber. These materials have thousands of microscopic pores that trap bacteria and can spread disease. The other types are easily cleaned with regular soap and water, or alcohol wipes if you want to be really safe. It goes without saying that all of the toys we'll be demonstrating here tonight use the safe, non-porous materials, so feel free to experiment away!"

As the women passed the little vibrators around the circle, some of them held it in their hands experiencing the different vibrations, while others pressed it gently between their legs as their eyes widened in surprise.

"Pretty powerful for such a little device, isn't it?" Cheryl said, nodding toward the more adventurous ladies. "But this is really just the most basic of sex toys. There's been a surge of innovative new designs to hit the market over the last couple of years."

She reached down into her case and picked up a donut-sized device with two pointy ends that looked like rabbit ears.

"This is the *Form 2* clitoral vibrator made by JimmyJane. The lovely thing about this sex toy is that you can place these two little fingers on opposite sides of the shaft of your clit to receive a heavenly stimulation, almost as if someone is stroking you with their hand. It's got a quiet but powerful internal motor that you can quickly recharge using the available charging cable. Unlike the pocket rocket, which uses a regular double-A battery. So you'll need to keep plenty of replacement batteries on hand to be sure you don't run out of power at the worst possible time."

Cheryl handed two models of the Form 2 vibe to me and I passed them to the girls in the middle of the circle.

"This one is best appreciated with a minimum of layers between you and the device," I hinted.

I nonchalantly unzipped my jeans and pulled them down to the floor, then slipped my own Form 2 vibe under my panties. A few of the girls raised an eyebrow at my bold gesture, but it didn't take long for them to refocus their gaze at my midsection as they watched me squirm and grunt from the pleasant sensations emanating between my legs.

Most of the other women were also wearing jeans and were reluctant to drop their leggings as they pressed the vibe gently against the seam of their pants. But a few had come prepared with skirts and summer dresses, and I watched excitedly as they slipped the two-pronged device under their hems and began to moan in pleasure. Unfortunately, nobody seemed quite ready to carry their self-stimulation to the ultimate peak and come in full view of the others as they politely passed the two devices around the circle.

Recognizing their hesitation, Cheryl reached into her toy case and pulled out another vibrator. This one looked like a small egg with two grooves on top and a little O-shaped loop connected to the end. She slipped her index and middle fingers through the loop and cradled the egg in the palm of her hand with her two fingers resting inside the grooves.

"This interesting device is called the *Fin*, manufactured by Dame Products, a female-founded and female-run adult toy company. The nice thing about this vibrator is that you can use it almost like an extension of your own hand. It's great to use in couples play to bring an extra level of stimulation to your partner. It's also equipped with a rechargeable battery and provides a quite satisfying sensation to the outer clitoris and overall vulva area. I happen to have four of these on hand, so I'm going to pass these around for more of you to enjoy."

Cheryl handed another one to me and smiled.

"As usual," she said, "Jade will be demonstrating some of the many ways you can use this for maximum enjoyment."

I placed the Form 2 vibrator over my hand then pressed my fingers under the top lip of my panties. As I felt the buzz spread over the head of my clit, I closed my eyes and spread my legs, sinking down in my chair. As I began to feel the rising tide of pleasure spread over my pelvic region, I opened my eyelids a slit and noticed three other women had unzipped the front of their jeans and had the palm of their hands gently rolling over their vulvas. As the rest of the girls squirmed in their seats looking on, the four of us mewed in obvious delight from the sublime tingling between our legs.

Feeling a bit sorry for the other girls being left out of the fun, I pulled the vibe out of my panties and tapped the button to turn it off.

"I'm saving myself for the *next* one," I winked. "I have a feeling Cheryl is getting ready to pull out the heavy guns."

Cheryl smiled at me as she reached into her case and pulled out a much larger device with a plum-sized ball attached to the end of a long handle.

"Right you are, Jade," she said. "This one has the generic name of magic wand and is made by various manufacturers, but my favorite version is this one with the trade name *Le Wand*. This is a major league vibrator, with a deep, penetrating rumble and twenty different vibration settings. It's not to be taken lightly, as it can set you off in a matter of seconds and can be quite addictive. You might want to be careful about pulling it out when your husband or boyfriend is around, since they might be more than a little threatened by both its size and how powerful it is."

Cheryl clutched the head of the device with her hand and twisted the round ball on the top.

"It's got a flexible neck, which makes it feel a bit more natural and it also comes with a bunch of fun attachments."

She reached into her bag and pulled out a variety of odd-shaped covers, placing each one over the end of the wand.

"This nubbly cover," she said, running her fingers over the spiny surface, "feels a bit like a French tickler when pressed against your vulva.

"Whereas *this* attachment," she said, replacing it with a cap having four large protruding nubs, "is billed as a deep tissue massager. But of course, it has much more interesting *sexual* exploration uses."

Then she reached into her case and pulled out a cone with a large curved finger extension.

"But this is my favorite attachment. It's perfectly shaped to stimulate the G-spot on the inside front surface of your vagina, and it will take you to an entirely different level. I'm going to hold off on passing this attachment around because we're going to have a special demonstration of the internal vibrators soon."

Cheryl turned to me with a devious smile.

"Jade, would you like to have first dibs at demonstrating this little gem?"

She passed me one of the wands and handed two others to the women at the edge of the circle.

"I thought you'd never ask," I said with a wicked grin.

"But this time I don't want anything getting between me and my vibrating friend. If you girls don't mind, I'm going to get buck-naked to properly enjoy this thing."

As many of the women around the circle widened their eyes in shock, I pulled my panties all the way down to my ankles. Then I flicked the switch on the side the wand and placed it against the front of my vulva, holding it with two hands.

"Fuck, yes!" I purred as the vibrator began to rumble between my legs.

I noticed it was starting to get dark outside and glanced through the crack in my curtains, recognizing some movement on the balcony across from my back yard. Just as I'd suspected, my neighbor Alana couldn't resist spying on me to get a closer look at what was going on inside. I couldn't tell if she was holding her binoculars, but I spread my legs as wide as I could as I rubbed the bat-shaped vibrator between my legs. If she was watching, I planned to give her a show she'd not soon forget.

Suddenly, I heard some moaning coming from the other ends of the circle and I turned my head to see the other women had thrust their magic wands down under their panties and were gripping the handle tightly as they rolled their hips sensuously in their chairs. I locked eyes on one of the girls, a married friend who'd previously been reluctant to share details about her sex life with her husband. As Heather and I began to feel the swell of pleasure sweeping over our bodies, we grunted and groaned in delirious pleasure.

Most of the other women who were without a vibrator had already shoved their hands down their pants or under their skirts as they watched the three of us tremble in our chairs. When Heather gaped her mouth wide open and began to shake uncontrollably in her chair, I couldn't hold back any longer. My orgasm overtook me and I grunted loudly as I hunched over, convulsing in ecstasy. Suddenly, the room was filled with the soft sighs and moans of twenty oversexed women losing themselves in the pleasure of intense self-stimulation as we watched each other rise to the culmination of pleasure.

3

———————

Seconds after I came, the doorbell rang. I was tempted to ignore it, but the interruption provided a welcome distraction from the awkwardness of twenty women peering at one another with their hands still down their pants. I threw on a robe and scampered up to the front door and looked through the peephole. It was my neighbor Alana, fidgeting self-consciously on the doorstep. I smiled for a moment, then swung open the door.

"Sorry I'm late," Alana stammered, staring at my curvy body wrapped up in the robe. "I had to finish making dinner and cleaning up after my husband. Have I missed much?"

I looked down at the wet patch in the crotch of her jeans and knew that she'd been touching herself as she watched me through the drapes.

"Not much," I said. "Come on in. We're just getting started."

I led Alana back to my family room and pulled up an extra chair at the edge of the circle.

"This is my neighbor Alana," I said, not wanting to interrupt our flow with a long introduction. "She was held up with a few unavoidable distractions, but better late than never to our party."

I motioned toward Cheryl, who was cleaning the wand I'd just used with an alcohol swab.

"This is my friend Cheryl from the Babeland store in downtown Chicago. She's been demonstrating some of the latest offerings from her establishment. Make yourself comfortable. We were just starting to get to the interesting items."

I looked at Cheryl and smiled.

"What other exciting toys have you got in that magic box of yours?"

"I'm glad you asked, Jade," Cheryl said. "I was just getting ready to demonstrate our line of *internal* vibrators."

She reached down into her case and lifted up two familiar-looking dildos. One had the traditional shape of a pointy pink cucumber and the other looked like an oversize erect penis.

"Until recently, these were the only kinds of internal vibrators that women had to choose from. One's shaped a bit like a pickle and is made out of hard plastic. The other one looks like a super-veiny cock, and is made out of soft silicone. While both come equipped with a handy internal vibrator, their designs are not very inspiring and, just like a man's cock, have limited functionality."

The lesbians around the circle chuckled, but more than a few of my straight friends also nodded, acknowledging their dissatisfaction with their one-dimensional sex lives. I glanced at Alana and she smiled at me nervously as a light blush spread over her cheeks.

Cheryl placed the vibrators back in her case then lifted

up another dildo shaped like a banana with a little bump on the end.

"This is called the *Gigi* vibrator, from Lelo," she said. She turned the device slowly in her hand, stroking the tip teasingly. "It has a gentle curve and a specially shaped tip that makes it perfect for stimulating the G-spot."

Cheryl looked toward Hannah and smiled.

"Hannah, would you like to demonstrate how to properly position this device using your little puppet?"

Hannah lifted her stuffed toy off the floor then slowly inserted the curved vibrator into the puppet's hole with the little bump facing up. Then she pressed the shaft downward, angling the tip toward the inside front surface of the vagina.

"As you can see," Cheryl said, "this vibrator is much better suited to stimulating the sensitive G-spot than a straight dildo. And the best part is that it's whisper-quiet, so you can use it discreetly in the privacy of your own bedroom without your husbands being any the wiser. Some women find it's easier to insert with a bit of lube, so we've placed a tube of body-safe cream beside everyone's chair if you want to give it a try."

As before, Cheryl passed one of the vibrators to me and three other girls in the circle. The women turned the wand curiously in their hands as they experimented with the different vibration settings, not quite ready to plunge it into their pussy in full view of the other participants.

Recognizing their apprehension, I flipped open my robe and spread my legs apart. I glanced over at Alana and noticed she had her legs crossed as she squeezed her thighs together while staring at me with wide eyes.

"I don't know about the *rest* of you," I grinned. "But I'm

still pretty wet from using the last vibrator. Screw the lube—I'm ready to get *fucked*."

I inserted the dildo deep into my pussy and angled it upward, then turned the vibration setting up all the way.

"Holy shit!" I growled. "This feels absolutely heavenly. You girls have *got* to give this a try. Remember, what happens in Jade's house, stays in Jade's house. We're all big girls and this can stay between us. No one else needs to know how much fun we really had at our little sorority party. Feel free to take off your pants and dresses and get your groove on!"

Two of the women holding the Gigi vibrator looked at one another for a moment, then they pulled their jeans down simultaneously, inserting the wand between their lips. They pressed the shaft in about four inches and angled it downwards as their eyes rolled under their lids and they slithered down in their chairs. I looked at the third woman, who'd slipped the vibrator under her dress, concealing it under her panties. But within seconds, all three of them began moaning and panting as they grasped the handle of the wand and thrust it firmly inside their pussies. I glanced at Alana, who had her hand down the front of her pants as the stain on her jeans spread further down her thighs.

The sight of so many women playing with themselves as they watched our glistening dildos plunging in and out of our pussies raised my excitement to an entirely new level, and I moaned loudly as I began to feel my passion rising. Within minutes, the four of us were trembling in our chairs as we watched each other fuck ourselves with this magnificent tool. As I began to feel the familiar tingling feeling spreading throughout my pelvic region, I spread my legs further apart and began to groan uncontrollably.

"Fuck—that feels so good," I said, shifting my gaze

between the three women. "I'm going to cum soon. Are you girls getting close?"

They all nodded as their moans began to rise with a heightened urgency and their eyes glazed over. When one of the girls suddenly slumped over in her chair and pulled her legs together, shaking convulsively, I groaned as I felt the contractions inside my pussy clamping against the shaft of the vibrator.

"I'm cumming!" I hissed, pulling the vibrator hard up inside me, pressing it firmly against the front of my cunny.

"Yes—Yes!" one of the other girls panted as she also began to quake in her chair.

But I was most turned on by the sight of the girl in the summer dress shaking in her chair as her mouth silently spread open and a deep rash washed over the top of her chest. By now, Alana was rubbing her clit furiously under the front of her jeans, and it didn't take long for her to slump forward, trying unsuccessfully to conceal the look of ecstasy on her face. Even Cheryl and Hannah were getting in on the action as they plunged their fingers deep inside their pussies.

After we all came down from our highs, Cheryl composed herself and sat back up in her chair.

"I knew you guys would enjoy that one," she said, trying to collect her breath. She panned around the room and made a mental note of who still hadn't had a chance to use one of the sex toys. "I see there's still a few of you who've been left out of the fun. Let's see if this next one might entice you into the fold, in a manner of speaking."

She reached down into her bag and lifted up another large penis-shaped dildo. But this time, two projections looking like little fingers protruded from the device about halfway up the shaft.

"Some of you ladies might recognize this little baby made famous by Samantha on Sex in the City. It's called the *Rabbit* because of these cute little ears that stick out from the side of the vibrator. But this device can stimulate you in so many other ways."

She flipped on the switch at the base of the unit and little chrome-colored beads began circulating around the middle of the translucent shaft. "These rotating balls provide quite a lovely sensation when you have it inserted inside you." She flicked another switch and the tip of the vibrator began rolling like a bobble head. "This vibrator might not be curved like the *Gigi*, but if you angle it properly inside your vagina, the twisting head does almost as good a job stimulating your G-spot."

Many of the women around the circle nodded, having had first-hand experience with the toy.

"But the best thing about this vibrator are these little rabbit ears," Cheryl said, flicking the two flexible flaps on the side of the device. "If you place them directly over your nub, you can get a full-body orgasm from the simultaneous stimulation of your inner and external clitoris. There's a reason why this is a staple in just about every woman's bedroom—it's the definitive multipurpose dildo for today's liberated woman. I've got two more of these to share with the girls who haven't yet had a turn, and I know Jade also keeps one of her own in her private collection."

I smiled at Cheryl as I pulled my brightly colored rabbit vibrator out of my bag resting on the floor.

"Damn straight, girl," I said. "This is my number one vibrator whenever I go on vacation, and I also keep it handy in the night table right beside my bed. This little guy has given me many an intense orgasm over the years. It's quite a special little toy. Although in this case—" I smirked, stroking the shaft, "it's not so *little*."

The girls laughed as I switched on my Rabbit and it began to whirl and roll like some kind of possessed robot-cock. Cheryl handed the other two vibrators to the women near the middle of the group, and I was disappointed not to see one of them passed to Alana. But I knew we still had a couple more toys to show, and I was confident that by the end of the evening she'd be fully participating like the rest of the girls. I was glad to see another one of my straight girl-friends holding one of the rabbit vibrators in her hand, and she looked at me devilishly as she smiled with a wide grin.

"You might want to use a bit of lube with this one," I said, looking at my gyrating vibrator in mock trepidation. "It's considerably bigger and girthier than the others, and you might find it slides in a little easier with a bit of help."

I picked up my tube of lube on the floor and squirted a healthy dollop up and down the shaft of the device, placing a few extra drops on the wide head. Then I placed the dildo between my legs and ran it up and down the inside of my labia to entice the other women to take off their clothes. Within seconds, the other two women had taken off their jeans and panties and were mimicking the movement of the dildo between their legs. As I watched their chests begin-ning to rise and fall in pleasure, I inserted my Rabbit into my hole and slowly pressed it further inside until the rabbit ears rested against my clit. When I felt the fingers trilling against my button, I sloped down in my chair, grasping the end of the dildo with two hands.

"This is one hell of a magic cock, don't you think ladies?" I grinned. "Who needs a man when you've got one of these to play with."

By now the other two women had inserted their Rabbits

deep into their pussies and were nodding vigorously in agreement. The sight of two big vibrating dildos planted deep inside their snatches was an incredible turn-on, and by now almost all the other women had removed their clothing and were jilling themselves unabashedly as they watched the three of us fucking ourselves with our big vibrating cocks. I glanced over at Alana and saw that her jeans were now resting around the base of her ankles with her fingers rotating under the front of her panties. I smiled at her and nodded, moaning approvingly at her loosening inhibitions.

I was still buzzing from my last orgasm, and it didn't take long for the feeling of impending climax to spread over my body as I watched the rest of the girls grunting in their chairs. But this time I didn't want to come so fast that I couldn't enjoy everybody else's experience to the fullest. I bit my lip and pulled the vibrator slightly away from my clit, concentrating on the feeling of the rotating beads and gyrating head moving inside me.

I wasn't sure if the other two girls had used a Rabbit before, but from the expression on their faces, they looked like they were having a transcendental experience. As their passion began to rise, I watched their bodies progressively tense up as they gripped the shaft of their big dildos with two hands and pulled it harder against their vulvas. I could see the rabbit ears flapping against their clits as they thrust the vibrating cock harder and harder inside their pussies until they both began to whine at the onset of a powerful orgasm.

"That's right," I encouraged, "let it go, girls. Let me watch you cum all over your big dildos. I'm going to cum with you."

Suddenly, the three of us wailed out loud as a powerful orgasm washed over us while we held the big dildos tightly against our vulvas, our legs stretched out in front of us, convulsing in a long simultaneous orgasm. I heard a squeal coming from the other end of the circle and I turned my head just in time to see Alana thrusting her fingers deep inside her cunny as she mimicked our action, lost in her own powerful orgasm. I smiled at her as we both shook deliriously in our chairs.

4

I t was hard to imagine getting any higher than this from any other of Cheryl's toys, but she smiled at me with a devious grin as she pulled her dripping fingers out of her panties. I was a little disappointed that she hadn't yet removed all of her clothes like most of the other ladies, but I guessed she wanted to maintain some degree of modesty while she continued her demonstration. After pausing a while for everyone to recover from their last episode, she reached down into her case and lifted up a U-shaped device with two flattened ends.

"I know you're all probably thinking it can't possibly get any more intense than that," she said. "But I've been saving the best for last. This interesting little device was developed by a woman who wanted to feel something different from the typical vibrator. It's called the *Osé*, by Lora DiCarlo. Unlike just about every other sex toy, this one doesn't have a conventional vibrating motor. Instead, it *undulates*, mimicking the feeling of a human touch on your vulva."

She turned on the device and it began to writhe in her hand like an animated snake.

"This end of the device flexes in a *come-hither* motion as if your partner is drawing his or her fingers gently against the inside of your G-spot.

Every woman, including myself, leaned in and squinted their eyes, mesmerized by the unusual movement of the toy.

"At the same time," Cheryl continued, "this end of the device slithers with a *pulsing* motion that mimics the feeling of a tongue licking the glans and shaft of your outer clit."

"Holy shit!" I said, shocked at the innovative design of the toy.

Cheryl turned her head toward me and nodded.

"Even *Jade* hasn't tried this one yet. It's just literally come onto the market and we're one of the few stores to be given exclusive distribution rights. Since none of you have tried it yet, I'm going to take the liberty of showing you how it works *myself* before I hand out a few extra models."

Cheryl lifted her hips off her chair and slipped her panties down to the floor, then raised her feet to shed the lower half of her clothes.

"As you can see," she said, holding the device directly in front of her separated legs. "This toy is shaped in the form of a 'U' and can be used hands-free once properly inserted. The fatter end goes inside and the thinner part rests on top of your outer clit."

She angled the device so the bottom of the U was facing the circle of women, then she inserted one end into her hole. As she gently pressed it upward, the thinner end slid up her vulva until it rested firmly over her clitoral shaft.

"There are two buttons on the bottom edge of the Osé that you can use to easily adjust the pace of the undulations."

She placed two fingers on the bottom of the U and tapped each one in turn.

"The button with the *Plus* symbol on the right-hand side increases the speed and the button with the *Minus* symbol beside it lowers the speed. But you won't notice a buzzing or throbbing sensation like the other vibrators. The buttons simply change the pace and rhythm of the undulations, much like your partner does when he or she adjusts the way they're licking and stroking you."

I could hear a gentle hum emanating from between Cheryl's legs as she spread her thighs apart and closed her eyes, concentrating on the feelings inside her.

"Before I get too lost in the pleasure provided by this incredible toy," she said, briefly opening her eyes, "I'm going to pass out three more models to the group. Please hand them along to those who haven't yet had a chance to test one of our vibrators. If I'm doing my math right, this last toy should cover the remaining girls who haven't yet had a try. But don't worry, ladies—you'll be glad you saved yourself until the end. This is one amazing sex toy that you won't soon forget."

Cheryl handed me three Osé toys, and I passed one to Alana and one to my straight friend Barb, keeping the last one for myself.

"You know what might be kind of fun this time," I smiled, noticing a few of the girls still partially covered up. "Is if we remove *all* of our clothing so we can watch and enjoy each other fully unencumbered with any camouflage. I don't know about the rest of you guys, but I get just as turned on *watching* your bodies as I do by touching myself. If you're all feeling comfortable enough, let's shed the rest of our trappings and revel in the beauty of our feminine bodies!"

It didn't take long for every single woman around the room to take off the last vestiges of their clothing. Even

Alana had dispensed with the last of her inhibitions as she pulled off her blouse and unclasped her bra behind her back. I panned around the semicircle, admiring the different shapes and sizes of all the sexy women.

"Let's get started then, shall we?" I said, winking at my friends.

Some of the girls still had a few of the earlier models of the sex toys resting beside their chairs and they picked them up as the three of us began to insert the curved Osé into our pussies. Those who didn't have access to a toy spread their legs wide apart and began to massage their clits with their fingers.

It felt strange slipping the unusual-shaped device inside my pussy, but as I pressed it further and further inside me, I hummed in satisfaction at the way it gripped my crotch. I almost felt like someone was cupping their hand over my vulva with their fingers touching my G-spot on the inside and their thumb resting over my clit on the outside. But when I tapped the On button at the base of the device, my eyes flew open in surprise.

Just as Cheryl had suggested, the sensation was unlike any other vibrator I'd previously used. Instead of a concentrated vibration sensation, the two ends of the device rolled and undulated against my tissues in a most natural way. On the inside, the long end curved and stroked me in a come-hither motion. On the outside, the other end undulated over my bulb, teasing and caressing my clit with its animated tongue-like action. I looked at the other two girls who had the Osé embedded in their pussies, and they had an equally incredulous expression on their faces.

I smiled at Alana, and she responded by spreading her legs further apart. I noticed the juices coating the inside of her thighs as she rolled her hips sensuously on her chair and locked eyes with me. The otherworldly feeling of someone touching me in my most sensitive areas was driving me insane, and for a brief moment, I fantasized about our two bodies pressed together so we could enjoy the feeling in unison. I knew this was likely the first time she'd had sex openly in the presence of other women, and it didn't take long for her to begin thrashing and moaning as she watched me and the other girls enjoying themselves. After only a few minutes of stimulation from her new sex toy, she suddenly threw her head back and screamed as her thighs began flapping together from the intense contractions washing over her. Not long after, Barb groaned equally loud as she shook violently in her chair from the orgasm taking control of her.

Within seconds, virtually everyone around the room including Cheryl and Hannah were squealing and shaking from the most erotic show any of us had ever witnessed. I was the last one to shoot off, and as I grabbed each of my tits in my hands, I gushed all the juices that I'd been building up inside my pussy out the two sides of my ring all over Cheryl and Barb, sitting directly in front of me. I sat convulsing in my chair for almost a full sixty seconds as the rest of the women watched in amazement. When I finally slumped forward in my chair, completely spent and exhausted, everyone stood up and clapped with a standing ovation.

5

After the three of us who'd used the Osé vibrator had come down from our highs, everybody looked at one another wondering what to do next. We were all dripping wet and buck naked, and nobody was in a hurry to end the party. But Cheryl had shared with me how she planned to step up each activity, and I knew she had one last trick up her sleeve that would bring everyone together in the end.

"That was fun, wasn't it?" she said, breaking the awkward silence. "It looked like some of you shared a pretty intense connection during that last demonstration. With that idea in mind, I had a few more toys to show you that were specially designed for multiple partner enjoyment."

She suddenly stood up and walked behind the sofa positioned against the far wall. She lifted an ottoman-sized object draped in a bedsheet off the floor and placed it in the center of the arc between the main group and our two chairs. Then she pulled off the cover with a flourish and threw it behind her. The device looked like a squat pommel horse, but in place of a saddle in the middle of the curved midsection were two diamond-shaped dildos pointing up about one foot apart.

"This strange contraption," Cheryl said, "is the *Sybian Sex Machine*, and it delivers quite a ride. It can be used by one or two people at a time, but as you can see from the double dildos positioned on top, it's best enjoyed as a partnered activity. Each person can face one another and caress the other as they receive powerful internal stimulation from the uniquely shaped dildos. The secure base of the unit allows both participants to ride the machine cow-girl style."

I panned around the circle and noticed the women looking at the device slack-jawed with wide eyes. It was obvious that few of them had seen or tried anything like it, but their erect nipples and swiveling hips suggested they were eager to give it a try.

"Those of you who like to have sex with a man once in a while," Cheryl smiled, "know that the girl-on-top position during intercourse allows for better control and provides a nice firm surface to rub your clits on. You'll notice this device comes with a vibrating pad under each dildo that delivers full-body stimulation to your entire vulva region. You really have to try it to appreciate it. Who'd like to volunteer to be our first test subjects?"

A few girls raised their arms and Cheryl pointed toward two women she recognized from their earlier trips into her store with their husbands. I was unsure if she purposely chose two straight girls to help break down their inhibitions about trying same-sex lovemaking, but I was nevertheless thrilled to see Dawn and Julie approach the device. They both had tight, athletic figures and I'd long fantasized about fucking one or both of them whenever we'd been out on group playdates together. I crossed my arms over my chest and pinched my nipples as I rubbed my legs together in anticipation of watching the two girls try the sexy machine.

"All you have to do is straddle the device," Cheryl instructed, leaning back in her chair holding a control box wired to the base of the unit. "Then sit down gently as you ease the dildos inside of you, facing one another. You might want to place a little lube on them first to make it go in a little easier."

She handed each woman a tube of lube and they generously lathered the dildos underneath them before sitting down over the plugs. The sight of the glistening phalluses disappearing into their neatly shaved snatches made the hairs on the side of my arms stand up on end. Suddenly I became aware of how wet my chair cushion had become as I watched the two women.

"How does that feel?" Cheryl said to the women.

They both made a soft mewing sound as they peered silently at Cheryl, afraid to look at one another and acknowledge that their naked bodies were mere inches apart.

"Can you feel the bulge in the middle of the plugs?" she asked. "They're designed to provide better stimulation of your G-spot once the action gets going."

"Um-hmm," Dawn nodded.

"Yup," Julie replied curtly.

"Let's see if we can make it a little more interesting," Cheryl said as she began to twist one of the dials on the control box.

A soft hum began to emanate from inside the machine, and the two women's eyes widened as they began to roll their hips unconsciously over the seat.

"Better?" Cheryl asked.

"Yes," Dawn panted, closing her eyes to concentrate on the buzzing feeling inside her.

"We've only *begun* to experience what this device can do," Cheryl winked.

She turned another knob on the control box, and the pads under the base of the dildos began to flap against the girls' clits. Julie gasped as she placed her hands behind her on the bench, unsure where to put her arms. Dawn crossed her arms nervously over her chest as she grunted and flitted her eyelids in pleasure.

"Feel free to touch one another," Cheryl said, trying to get the girls to loosen up and become more engaged with one another. "The whole point of this device is to revel in each other's pleasure and make it an interactive experience."

Dawn reached out tentatively and cupped each of Julie's trembling tits in her palms. Julie leaned forward and placed her arms around Dawn's back then the two women pressed their bodies together.

"There we go," Cheryl nodded. "Feel the pleasure coursing through each other's bodies as you caress one another. Lose yourself in the experience as you become one. We're going to begin ramping up the intensity level now."

She twisted both knobs further to the right then flicked a switch on the side. Each of the dildos suddenly began gyrating inside the women's pussies, pressing more firmly against the front of their tunnels. Both women groaned and locked lips, probing their tongues inside each other's mouths. As they began to mash their breasts together and moan in unison from the incredible sensation enveloping their pussies, I glanced around the room.

All the other women were playing with themselves in one form or another as they watched the sexy show in front of them. For my part, the sight of two straight girls rubbing their bodies together as they were being remotely stimu-lated by an innocent bystander was too much to resist. I picked up my rabbit vibrator off the floor and flicked the speed to max as I jammed it inside my pussy, pulling it hard against my tingling button.

"That's what I'm talking about," Cheryl purred, watching the two women beginning to lose themselves in each other's passion. "Are you ready to take it to the penultimate level?"

"Mmm-hmm," the two women nodded as they ran their hands over each other's bodies while they continued to kiss passionately.

Cheryl twisted the two dials to their maximum setting, and the hum inside the machine deepened as the flaps under their pussies began to flap wildly. Dawn and Julie pressed their hips forward, gyrating their hips together as they got closer and closer toward climax. Within seconds, they began wailing in tandem as their bodies shook violently with their arms clasped tightly around each other. Seeing the two women coming together soon put me over the edge also as my pussy clamped tightly over the vibrating shaft of my Rabbit toy. I glanced over at Alana and noticed that she was holding a Form 2 vibrator over her clit while she quaked in her chair watching the other women in the room jilling themselves as they took in the action.

6

———

After everyone had finished coming once again, Cheryl looked at the two girls still sitting on the now-silent Sybian machine.

"What do you think, ladies?" she said. "Does that feel anything like riding your husbands on top?"

"Fuck no!" Dawn said. "This is way better!"

Julie nodded enthusiastically in agreement, and everybody around the room laughed out loud.

"Well at least now you know how much fun it can be to play with some of your own kind," Cheryl said. "And while we're on that subject, I'd like to demonstrate a couple of toys that will allow you to be even *more* actively engaged with your same-sex partners." She peered at Dawn and Julie and smiled. "You guys are welcome to stay there if you wish or return to your seats for this next demonstration."

The two women kissed each other one last time then eased themselves off the bench, revealing two glistening, pearly-white dildos. When they returned to their seats, I noticed they were holding hands beside one another. I smiled at their new special friendship and nodded at them approvingly.

Cheryl moved the Sybian machine off to the side of the circle then reached back down into her display case. When she sat up, she revealed a giant flexible dildo with a raised ring running around the middle of the shaft.

"This is a two-sided or double dildo," she said, running her fingers over the two ends of the object shaped in the form of the head of a man's penis. "As you can see, it's a little longer than a regular man's cock and it has two heads for double the pleasure. Perhaps *most* interesting though, is this raised band in the middle."

She squeezed the shaft near the center and the band began flapping like the pads on the Sybian machine.

"When two women press this dildo inside them from opposite ends, the vibrating ring in the middle provides some very pleasant supplemental stimulation as they grind their pussies together. Unlike the Sybian machine, which you experience in more of a passive role, with this device you can actively fuck each other in a multitude of positions."

Cheryl looked around the room and smiled mischievously.

"Who'd like to give this one a try?"

Two of my lesbian friends raised their hands but I quickly pre-empted them. Watching Cheryl demonstrate her toys all this time had gotten me seriously worked up and I jumped at this opportunity to have some fun with her.

"I notice that *you* haven't yet had a chance to use any of your toys today, Cheryl," I said. "If you're game, I'd be happy to demonstrate this one for the rest of the group with your participation."

"I thought you'd never ask," Cheryl said, winking at me.

"Let's get down on the floor and show these ladies how two lesbian women can get it on."

I lay down on the carpet in front of the chairs with my hips facing up and spread my knees apart. Cheryl lay down in a similar position facing me, with our vulvas about a foot apart. Then she squirted a drop of lube on each end of the dildo and pressed one end against her opening. As she shimmied her hips toward me, half of the dildo slowly disappeared inside her pussy. When the other end pressed against my hole, I mimicked her movement until the plug was fully inserted inside our bodies with our vulvas mashed together.

"Are you *in* yet?" Cheryl joked, lifting her head off the floor and peering toward me.

"Judging by the feel of your wet pussy pressing against mine, I'd say so," I meowed.

"Shall we get started then?" she said.

"By all means," I purred.

As we both began rolling our hips together, I felt the dildo thrusting in and out of me as it plunged deeper and deeper inside my cunt. Although it wasn't vibrating yet and it didn't have the beneficial shape of some of the other curved vibrators, the feeling of Cheryl actively fucking me with the unicock and the sensation of her wet lips grinding against mine more than made up for the lack of other features.

Suddenly, she rolled over onto her side and straddled me with one leg under my ass and the other one over my tummy. As she humped me more aggressively, she began to grunt like a wild animal. I was enjoying the experience of being on the bottom for a change, but just as I began to feel the familiar feeling of another orgasm rising up within me, she turned over another ninety degrees until she was facing face-down on the carpet.

"Fuck me from behind, Jade," she groaned. "I want to feel your ass slapping against mine."

"Fuck yes!" I said, quickly rolling over so we were both facing down.

We pulled our knees forward and lifted ourselves up until we were resting on all-fours with our butt cheeks pressing against one another. Cheryl reached between her legs and pinched the middle of the dildo, and the snake suddenly began writhing inside our pussies as the ring between our legs flapped against our two clits.

"Oh God," I moaned as Cheryl began rocking her hips against me, slapping her ass against mine.

The simultaneous feeling of the gyrating dildo in my pussy with Cheryl's ass grinding against mine and the vibrating ring trembling against my burning clit felt incredible.

"*Fuck*, Cheryl," I hissed. "I'm gonna cum. I'm gonna cum so hard all over your pretty ass. Come with me baby."

"I'm close," Cheryl growled. "Spray all over my wet hole. Let me feel you cum all over my burning cunt."

Whether it was Cheryl's sexy dirty talk or the sensation of being watched by all the other women around the room, I felt my orgasm suddenly wash over me as I began to shake uncontrollably against Cheryl's ass. My pussy clamped down hard on the flexible dildo as I felt the juices squirting out of my hole all over her opening.

"Yes, Jade!" she wailed. "Spray me with your cum. I'm coming baby! Fill up my hole as you cum inside me!"

As we both pawed the carpet like two cats in heat, I heard the sighs of other women around me and turned my head to see every one of them fucking themselves with one device or another as they watched us, their breasts trembling as they came in simultaneous union with Cheryl and me.

7

———

As the two of us lay spent and exhausted on the floor, I looked up at the other women peering at one another expectantly. It was obvious that they were ready to engage more actively with some of the others, and this seemed like the ideal time to open things up for broader participation. Cheryl and I looked at each other, thinking the same thing, and nodded.

"This seems like a good time for the rest of you to find a partner and try some interactive play," I said. "Feel free to grab whatever toy you can find and experiment away. It's always a lot more fun when you bring someone else into the mix, and there's a limitless degree of combinations you can create when you bring other partners into the equation. Grab a spot on the sofa, or use one of my private rooms, or join the rest of us on the floor. This party is a long way from being over!"

Almost immediately, all the other girls joined us on the floor, pairing up with new and old acquaintances, as they picked up various loose toys and rubbing them against each other's bodies. I peered over in Alana's direction and noticed that she was sitting by herself, looking at my naked body longingly. I turned to Cheryl, still joined at the hips with me on the floor, and she motioned for me to go to her. I pulled myself off my half of the dildo and Hannah quickly took my place, smiling at Cheryl as they pressed their hips together.

I was happy to see my friends hooking up and enjoying themselves so openly, but as I walked toward Alana crossing her legs shyly, I felt sorry for the one person in the group who still seemed hesitant to participate in the group fun.

"Haven't you been enjoying the party?" I said, taking a seat on the chair beside her.

"Yes, of course," Alana said, placing her arms shyly over her chest.

"I've noticed you participating at various times," I smiled. "But you seem reluctant to engage with the others. Are you feeling uncomfortable?"

"No—not really," she said. "It's just that no one else here...*interests* me."

I sensed what Alana was getting at, but I wanted to be sure before taking the next step.

"No one else meaning..."

"*You*, Jade," she said, peering into my eyes. "I've been watching you for so long, wanting to make love to you."

I slipped off my chair and kneeled in front of her, kissing her softly on her lips.

"I've been watching you from afar also, Alana," I said. "I've had many a sleepless night fantasizing about your beautiful figure, imagining myself touching and licking your naked body."

I lowered myself down the front of her body, nibbling the side of her neck and kissing the top of her chest. When I reached her firm breasts, I cupped each one in my hands and ran my tongue over her nipples in gentle circles. I could feel her nubs hardening in my mouth as I sucked on them gently. Alana tilted her head back and moaned, pressing her body toward me. As I moved in closer, she spread her legs further apart, and I could feel the heat emanating from her pussy.

Eager to feel her in my mouth, I continued lower until my face was level with her mound. I was a little surprised to find her so smooth and bare down there, and I looked up at her with a quizzical look.

"I shaved myself just for you," she said. "I didn't want anything coming between the two of us tonight."

I smiled up at her then rolled my cheeks against her soft pubis, flapping my eyelids with butterfly kisses against her skin as her thighs trembled in anticipation of my touch further below.

"Suck me, Jade," Alana whinnied, pressing her hips harder toward me. "I want to feel your lips on my most private parts. I've been dreaming about this for so long—"

Before she could finish her sentence, I lowered my face and encircled her flaming clit in my mouth, rolling my tongue over her pearl. Alana gasped and grabbed the back of my head, pulling me harder against her soaking vulva. I hummed in approval, alternating between flicking my tongue over her erect shaft and sucking her button deeply into my mouth. Her clit was larger than most, and I could feel her sex extend a full inch into my mouth as I sucked on her little cocklet.

Alana began rocking her hips wildly on her chair as she fucked my mouth shamelessly. Her groans grew progressively louder but just as I was sure she was about to come in my mouth, she suddenly pulled away and peered down at me with a possessed look on her face.

"I want to feel you inside me when I cum," she said.

"Fuck me, Jade. Fuck me with one of Cheryl's sexy toys. I want to be your bitch."

I shook my head in shock, momentarily taken aback by Alana's newfound boldness. Whether this was simply her straight side wanting to get fucked in the manner she was accustomed to, or she was demonstrating her desire to adopt the femme persona in our new lesbian tryst, I didn't care. I just wanted to take her and consummate our long, lingering relationship as quickly as I could. My eyes darted along the floor to find something I could fuck her with, but seeing that all the other toys were in use by the other women engaged in heated affairs, I peered into Cheryl's case and noticed a strap-on dildo.

"Wait here, babe," I said. "I think I have just the thing."

I walked gingerly around all the writhing bodies on the floor and reached slowly into her case. Hannah and Cheryl were nearing the point of no return as they fucked each other wildly with the two-ended dildo, and they smiled at me devilishly as my breasts wobbled above their faces.

"Go fuck that girl," Hannah said. "Show her what it's like to experience a real orgasm."

I nodded at her then scampered back to Alana's chair where I found her already kneeling on the floor with her glistening ass pointed up toward me.

"Yes, Jade," she purred. "Fuck me with that big dildo. Let me feel your big cock deep inside me."

It didn't take more than a few seconds to wrap the belt around my waist and legs to secure the big phallus over my mound. It had a gentle downward curve and a thick head specifically intended for G-spot stimulation when used from behind. I noticed a couple of buttons on the front of the harness, but I was in too much of a hurry to feel Alana's pussy wrapped around my cock to figure out what they did.

I reached between her legs to see if she needed any lubrication and she was slippery as a runny faucet. I pointed the tip of the dildo against her hole and wasted no time slamming it inside her cavern. If she wanted it rough, I thought, I was only too happy to oblige.

"Oh *fuck*!" Alana groaned. "That feels so good. Can you feel me squeezing you?"

I couldn't of course, because it was an artificial dildo. But I could feel the resistance of her tight pussy clamping against my faux cock as I pulled it out and slammed it back into her. The feeling of her ass cheeks slapping against my mound and my throbbing clit just amplified the feeling of fucking her like a man. I wondered what her husband would think if he knew what I was doing to his wife behind my closed curtains.

From her escalating moans and movements, I could tell that she was close to popping off, and I selfishly wanted to come with her. Maybe it was from me channeling the replacement of her husband or maybe it was just me desperately wanting to get off again. But either way, as sexy as it was to screw this little vixen with my artificial cock, I wasn't getting quite enough direct stimulation to get there with her.

I pulled out of her halfway for a moment and tapped a few of the buttons on the front of my harness. Suddenly, the dildo began throbbing with a deep rumble and another motor began vibrating against my nub under the harness.

"Holy shit," Alana hissed. "This thing is *way* better than my husband's cock. Whatever you're doing, it's driving me crazy. Fuck me harder, Jade. I'm getting close."

"So am I," I grunted, overwhelmed by the multiple sensations of fucking my neighbor from behind while simultaneously getting jilled on my clit. "Come with me baby. Let me feel you gushing all over my dick."

"Yes, Jade!" Alana cried. "Here it comes—I'm cumming!!"

Suddenly, I lost all sense of control as every ounce of my pent-up passion poured out of my body. As I began shuddering with intense contractions, I gushed my wetness out the sides of my harness down both sides of Alana's inner thighs. Feeling me cumming all over her, she wailed at the top of her lungs as her hips began shaking in spastic convulsions. I leaned over and squeezed her tits firmly with my hands as we both grunted in ecstatic union. When the two of us finished our long and intense climax and finally collapsed together on the floor, I noticed the rest of the girls lying beside us with silly grins on their faces.

This was one party none of us would soon forget.

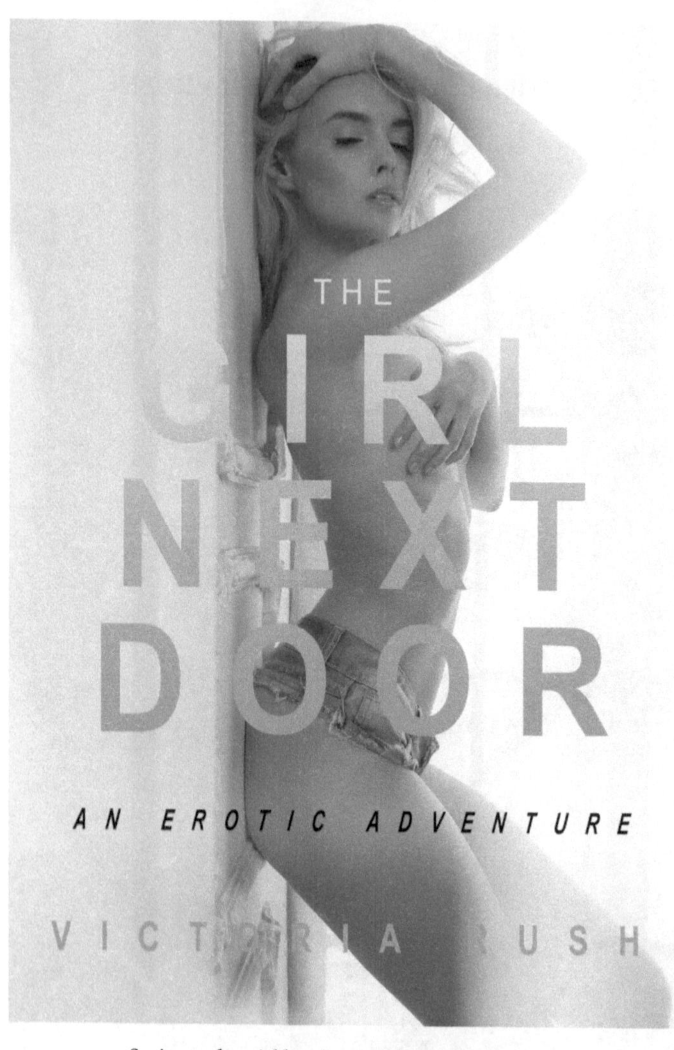

Spying on the neighbors just got a lot more interesting...

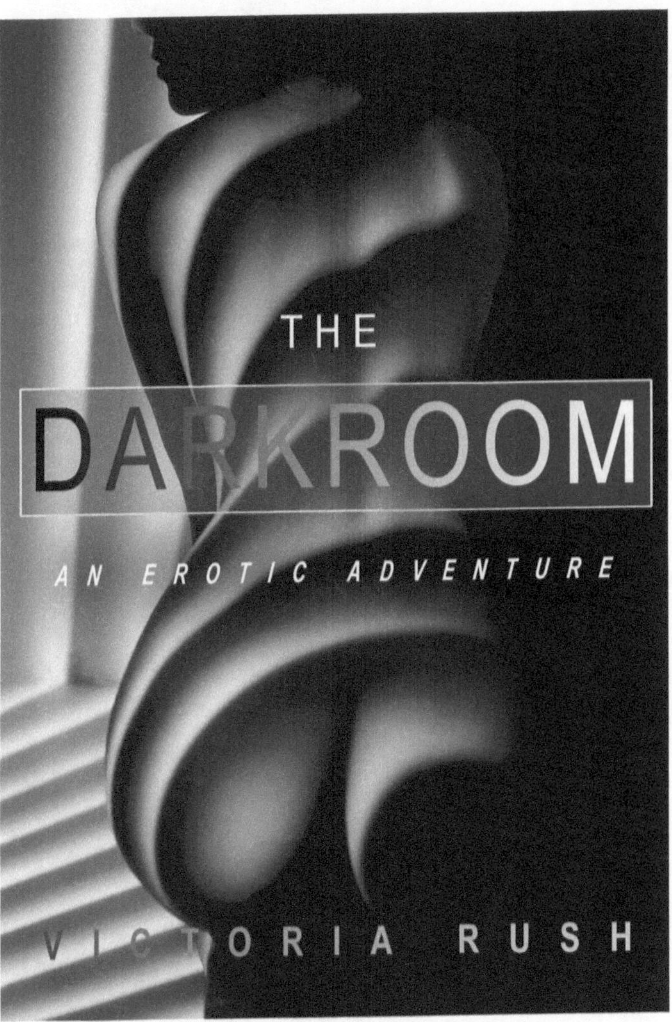

Everything's sexier in the dark...

Artificial intelligence never felt so real...

Books 6 - 10 in the bestselling series - now 60% off.

THE DINNER PARTY - PREVIEW
FINGER FOOD

Sometime later, I heard a soft tap on my bedroom door. Not wanting to remove myself just yet from my cocoon of luxury, I called out to answer.

"Yes?"

"It's time for your massage," a woman's voice replied.

"Just one minute please."

I reluctantly stepped out of the bath and quickly toweled myself dry. I wrapped a large bath sheet around me, re-donned my mask, then opened the bedroom door.

A petite young Asian girl greeted me, wearing a kimono similar to mine and a crimson masquerade mask.

Apparently not everybody who works here always walks around stark naked.

The girl was utterly breathtaking. Long jet-black hair cascaded over high cheekbones past pouty lips, her delicate collarbones peeking from the top of her kimono. I could see her breasts and hips outlined by the tightly-wrapped kimono and suddenly wished that she too had come to my boudoir naked.

"My name is Jasmine," she said. "I'm your personal

masseuse and esthetician. Are you ready for your final preparation?

Just the thought of this beauty laying her tender hands on me sent a shiver down my spine.

"Definitely. Please come in. How would you like me to prepare?"

"Come with me, please."

Jasmine led me into the bathroom, where she nonchalantly removed her kimono and hung it behind the bathroom door.

Oh my God.

I didn't think anyone in this place could get more beautiful or sensuous. Jasmine had perfectly shaped B-cup breasts with a thin indentation running down the center of her perfectly toned stomach. Like everyone else in this place, her pubis was utterly bald and flawless. She barely looked eighteen and I was just about to ask her age, but she spoke first.

"If you'd like to remove your towel and lay face down on the table, we can get started. May I call you Jade?"

There was something about her confident manner and tone that belied her youthful appearance. I had no inhibitions whatsoever about displaying myself unclothed to this stranger.

"Yes, thank you, Jasmine." I unhooked my bath sheet and threw it against the side of the tub.

"Would you like me to drape your backside?" Jasmine asked.

"That won't be necessary," I quickly answered.

Jasmine walked over to the vanity counter and picked up two small bottles of oil resting under an orange radiant lamp. She brought them back to the massage table, opened one, and poured the oil into one cupped hand then rubbed her hands together. The scent of lavender wafted toward my nose.

I closed my eyes in anticipation of her touch. I'd had massages before, but nothing as sensuous and stimulating as this. When her hands touched the small of my back, I jerked reflexively from the sexual tension. My heart was beating a hundred miles an hour as I felt the blood coursing through my veins.

Jasmine must have sensed my nervous tension and began pressing her fingers more firmly into my back as she moved them slowly up each side of my spine. The warm oil allowed her hands to glide effortlessly across my skin. She used every surface of her hands to massage my muscles, expertly kneading my skin with her fingers and palm.

I began to relax as my muscles softened and surrendered to her touch. She sensuously massaged every part of my back, shoulders, and neck, applying just the right amount of pressure. Periodically, she would pour more warm oil on my lower back, dipping her hands in it to replenish the silky lubrication against my pliant skin.

Just as the sexual tension began to subside from the utter relaxation of the massage, Jasmine moved her hands down to my buttocks and began to caress them in soft circular motions. My glutes contracted involuntarily and I unconsciously pressed my mound into the firm padding of the table. Suddenly I was quickly reminded that a gorgeous young woman was caressing my naked body. She cupped each buttock between her hands as she massaged my ass tantalizingly, her little finger sliding slowly into the cleft just above my anus.

Periodically, I'd partially open one of my eyes with my head turned in her direction to look at her gorgeous body. My head was at the same level as her midsection, and my mouth watered as I watched her stomach muscles flex and her hips undulate with each movement of her hands. At times her pussy was almost right beside me and I wanted to reach out and run my own fingers up her soft legs.

I was in total heaven and getting wetter by the moment. Just when I thought I couldn't stand it anymore, she suddenly moved her hands down to my feet and began massaging her thumbs into my soles.

I'd always loved having my feet massaged, but nobody did it like Jasmine. She cradled my foot and used every part of her hands to massage and knead every surface from my heel to my toes. I didn't want her to stop, but there were other parts of my body that were screaming for attention.

As if reading my thoughts, she began moving her hands up toward my calf, using her thumbs to spread the muscle apart. She lingered almost as long on my calf as she had on my foot, rolling the ball of my calf between both of her hands, sliding her slick hands up and down erotically. I couldn't help imagining how she might use those same hands to massage a man's erect cock in a similar manner. My mind wandered again to what pleasures lay in wait for me over dinner.

After shifting her hands to my right leg and giving my other foot and calf similar attention, she placed each hand just behind my knees and began to slowly move them up towards my buttocks. Her thumbs pressed against my inner thighs as she glided tantalizingly close to my apex.

I rolled my legs outward in an invitation to move closer. My legs were parted enough that I was sure she could see my vulva from her vantage point behind me. In my highly aroused state, my lips were engorged and spread apart, revealing my moist and quivering opening.

But as much as I desperately wanted her to, Jasmine

never touched me there. She repeatedly slid her hands right up to the edge of my slit, pressing and rotating her thumbs on the fleshy meat of my upper thighs just below my aching pussy. I suppose this was part of her master plan—to tease me mercilessly and inflame my passions so I'd be ready for just about anything at the main event.

It was certainly working. After thirty minutes of Jasmine's ministrations, I was grinding my pussy into the table trying desperately to give my clit some needed direct stimulation.

Just when I thought I couldn't be teased any more tantalizingly, Jasmine opened one of the bottles of warm oil and poured it directly into the crack of my ass. She paused as the fluid flowed down and directly over my parted lips. I almost came from the gentle movement of the warm liquid as it trickled across the folds of my labia, channeled toward the junction where they joined together at my clit. I shuddered in pleasure at the feeling, even if it was only the subtlest of touch.

Jasmine suddenly interrupted my thoughts.

"Would you like to turn over now?"

It was the first time she had spoken directly to me since the massage started, and it surprised me in my catatonic, pre-orgasmic state. I practically flipped over like a fish out of water and spread my legs expectantly. Finally, I'd get some relief. Surely, she couldn't leave me hanging like this.

"It's time for your final grooming," she said. "I'll need you to part your legs a bit further to provide full access."

Grooming? I knew this was part of the process, but somehow it didn't seem fair to transition at this precise moment. At least I'd be able to stay on the comfortable massage table instead of the clinical vinyl chairs used by my regular esthetician.

Jasmine walked over to another cabinet by the makeup table and withdrew a leather bag from one of the drawers, then brought it back to the table. She reached into the bag and pulled out a cordless hair trimmer.

"Do you have a preference regarding your appearance?" she asked. "Do you prefer natural, neatly trimmed, or bare?"

I knew she was referring to my pubic hair, which I generally kept neatly trimmed. I'd always thought going fully bald was unnatural and unseemly, catering to men's prurient fantasies of fucking young schoolgirls. But in this situation, it seemed entirely appropriate, like I was stripping away all my camouflage and armor.

If tonight was all about being watched, I might as well bare myself in every sense of the word and truly let my inhibitions go. I began to fantasize about rubbing my bare pussy against Jasmine's while she poured warm oil between us. The more work she had to do on me, the more chance I'd have to make this last and hopefully get off.

I didn't hesitate. "Bare, thank you."

"As you wish," she said. "I'll remove the long hairs first with the trimmer, then shave you smooth with a razor."

No waxing? This was different. I was relieved to not have to bear the painful and violent trial of having my hairs ripped out en masse. Although shaving down there was always a scary proposition, I felt safe in the capable and practiced hands of this beautiful esthetician.

Jasmine nodded, then flipped a switch on the trimmer. The device buzzed softly as she placed it gently on my mound. I had only a light dusting of fur and it didn't take long for her to remove it with a few short strokes over my pubis. I shuddered as the vibrations penetrated deep into my core. If she had placed the flat head on my clitoris, I would have popped off in a millisecond. Instead, she turned the trimmer face-down and gently swiped the vibrating teeth against the sides of my vulva, sensuously separating my labia with her hands as she moved the device between my legs to trim the hairs on the inside and outside of my labia.

It was an insanely titillating feeling, but just clinical enough to bring me down from my plateau and shift my focus. My mind wandered to the upcoming feast, and I contemplated what surprises lay in wait at the main event. The hostesses had suggested there would be 'contact' of some sort during the meal, and I was intrigued exactly who and how it would be administered. The idea of being fully bald, cleansed, and thoroughly stimulated going into the event was an incredible rush.

Jasmine continued with the trimmer all the way down my perineum to my anus, barely touching me with the trimmer so as not to pinch any delicate tissues. Apparently there were no parts of my erogenous zone that would remain untouched, now—and perhaps later.

She turned off the trimmer and placed it at the foot of the table. Then she took a bottle of gel from the bag and spread the gel on her hands. Using both hands, she spread it gently between my legs, starting on my mound all the way down to my rosebud.

My body almost levitated above the table as Jasmine finally laid her hands directly on my clitoris. The gel had a mild stinging quality that added to the stimulating sensation. If this was meant to excite my follicles in preparation for the shave, it wasn't the only feature of my anatomy that it made erect. I could feel the hood of my clitoris retract as my button filled with blood and began to push outward. Suddenly, I was fully stimulated again and lusting for Jasmine's touch. I fantasized about her bending down and taking my swollen nub between her puffy lips and letting me come in her mouth.

Unfortunately, my satisfaction would have to wait a little longer. Instead, Jasmine reached into her bag and pulled out a straight-edge razor. In anyone else's hands, it might look threatening, especially in my prostrated and vulnerable position. But something about the way she delicately and sensuously opened the jackknifed tool instantly evaporated my fears. I could see how this type of razor would in fact give her better control safely cutting my stubs instead of the usual ladies plastic razor.

With her right hand, Jasmine gently laid the razor on its flat edge at the top of my mound, while she gently pulled my skin upwards with her other hand. Then she slowly turned the sharp edge perpendicular to my skin and began softly scraping the razor downwards. I could hear the bristling sound as the razor edge removed my nubs right down to the follicles. She repeated the pattern in one inch wide swipes on one side then the other of my pubis, being ever-so-careful to stop just where my clitoris lay quivering in a mixture of fear and excitement. There was something about the utter vulnerability of the procedure that made it the most erotic experience I'd ever had.

Jasmine used the same deft touch as she moved down my vulva and perineum, scraping the vestiges of stray hairs away with gentle swipes of the long blade, while sensuously separating my folds and flesh with her other hand. She took extra time and care around my anus and clit, using the gentlest and slowest motion I've ever felt someone apply to my body. The combination of fright and titillation as she probed my most sensitive body parts created a river of sensuous fluids running down my vulva. By this time, no shaving gel was necessary to provide a smooth gliding surface for the knife.

When she was finished, Jasmine retrieved a fresh wash towel from beside the sink and held it under the warm water faucet then twisted the excess water into the basin. She returned to the table and placed it over my splayed legs then gently cleansed the excess moisture and remaining shaving gel with gentle massaging movements of her hands. The warm, moist towel felt exquisite against my newly shaved skin. Jasmine's hands now felt comforting between my legs rather than erotic.

She had taken me on an incredibly sensuous erotic arc, right to the edge of ecstasy and back, to a quiet relaxed place. I exhaled fully and completely for the first time in almost an hour.

Jasmine removed the towel from between my legs and held up a large hand mirror at a forty-five degree angle toward me.

"What do you think?" she asked.

I tilted my head up and studied her masterpiece. Far from the usual red and swollen vulva that I typically experienced after the violent waxing with my regular esthetician, I'd never seen my pussy look so beautiful. Utterly bereft of any hair, my entire perineum from my pubic mound to my anus was totally bald, pink—and gorgeous. I just stared at my beautiful pussy, utterly transfixed by the transformation.

"You have to *feel* it to really appreciate how beautiful you are, Jade," Jasmine purred.

I moved my right hand down, running my fingers along the edges of my pussy. I gasped from a feeling I'd never felt before. It felt smooth as silk: no bumps or blemishes or cuts or bruises. It was almost as if I was feeling somebody else— somebody I'd never felt before. I couldn't stop my left hand joining the other in rubbing and caressing my sensitive organs.

Jasmine lowered the mirror and smiled at me as I felt the moisture begin to accumulate between my legs again.

"It's almost time for your dinner appointment," she said. "Why don't you save the best for last? I think you'll find plenty of ways to satisfy your appetite over the next couple of hours."

She lifted my kimono from the hook at the edge of the bathtub and held it open for me.

"I'll escort you downstairs now if you're ready. All you need to bring is your kimono and slippers—and your mask of course."

I sat up slowly and stepped off the massage table. Turning around, I held my arms out as Jasmine lifted one arm of the silk robe onto me then the other. Then she turned around to face me, wrapped the silk tie around me, and tied a single bow over my belly button. She retrieved my matching silk slippers and knelt down on one knee to gently lift my feet one at a time and place them softly inside. It took every ounce of my power not to grab her head and pull it into my pulsating pussy.

Jasmine stood up gracefully and smiled into my eyes.

"If you'll follow me, I'll escort you now to the fantasy feast."

She didn't bother putting her own robe on. Her tight little ass barely jiggled as she stepped smartly ahead of me. I wasn't sure if I'd have a chance to feel Jasmine's touch again before the evening was over, but for now I was in total bliss ogling her petite, curvaceous figure from behind...

Read More

ABOUT THE AUTHOR

If you would like to receive notification of new book(s) in Jade's Erotic Adventures, follow me at http://bookbub.com/authors/victoria-rush.

If you have a moment, please post a brief review on my Amazon book page at viewbook.at/ttp . Even just a couple of sentences will help other readers find and enjoy this book as much as you hopefully did.

Follow, share, like, and comment at:

www.facebook.com/authorvictoriarush
www.pinterest.com/authorvictoriarush
www.twitter.com/authorvictoriarush
authorvictoriarush@outlook.com

Hope to see you again soon!

www.ingramcontent.com/pod-product-compliance
Lightning Source LLC
Chambersburg PA
CBHW030822200726
48288CB00004B/1348